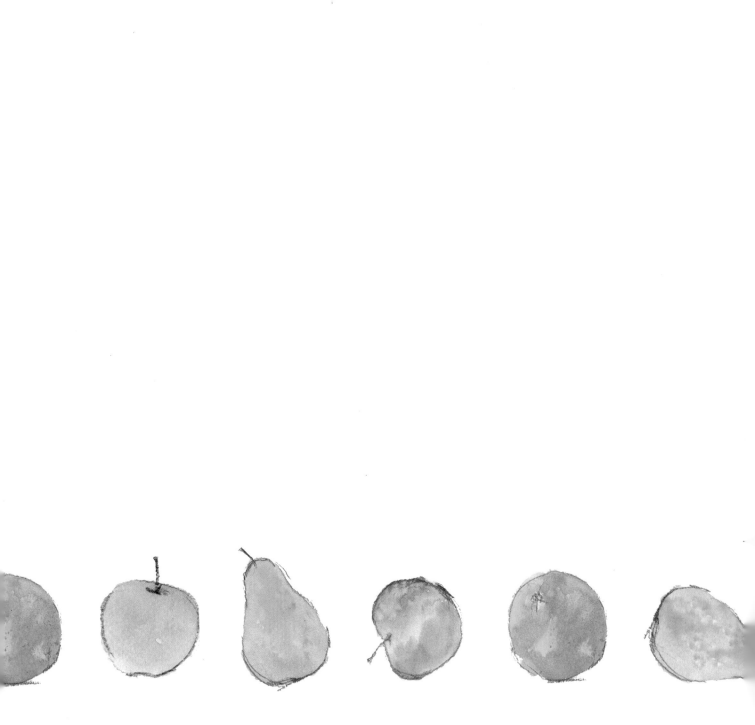

Orange
Pear
Apple
Bear

For Mik

SIMON & SCHUSTER BOOKS FOR YOUNG READERS
An imprint of Simon & Schuster Children's Publishing Division
1230 Avenue of the Americas, New York, New York 10020
Copyright © 2005 by Emily Gravett
First published in Great Britain in 2006 by Macmillan Children's Books
First U.S. edition 2007
Published by arrangement with Macmillan Children's Books
All rights reserved, including the right of reproduction in whole or in part in any form.
SIMON & SCHUSTER BOOKS FOR YOUNG READERS is a trademark of Simon & Schuster, Inc.
Manufactured in China
2 4 6 8 10 9 7 5 3 1
Library of Congress Cataloging-in-Publication Data
Gravett, Emily.
Orange pear apple bear / Emily Gravett—1st U.S. ed.
p. cm.
Summary: Explores concepts of color, shape, and food using only five simple words, as a
bear juggles and plays.
ISBN-13: 978-1-4169-3999-3
ISBN-10: 1-4169-3999-7
[1. Bears—Fiction. 2. Play on words—Fiction.]   I. Title.
PZ7.G77577Ora 2007
[E]—dc22
2006017964

Orange
Pear
Apple
Bear

Emily Gravett

Simon & Schuster Books for Young Readers
New York London Toronto Sydney

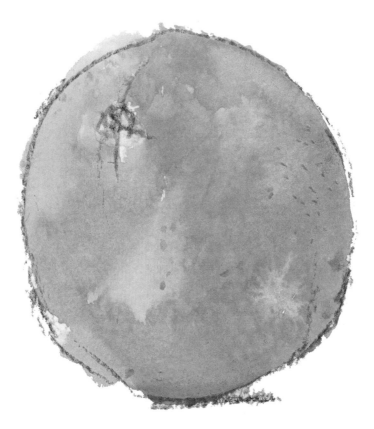

Orange

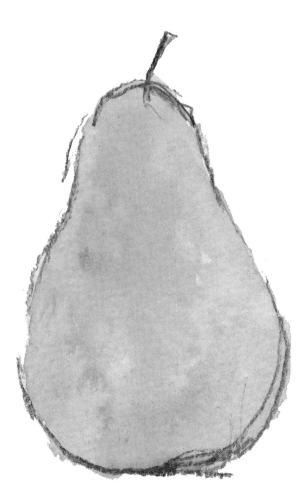

Pear

Apple

Bear

Apple, pear

Orange bear

Orange pear

Apple bear

Apple, orange, pear bear

Orange, pear, apple, bear

Apple,

bear,

orange,

pear

Orange, bear

Pear, bear

Apple, bear

There!